THE 10 PLAGUES OF 2020

ARIAL AVI

About the book

This book is going to be very controversial. I am in absolute awe and shock at the time of writing this chapter. I am not a doom monger but something is happening. Let me tell you the good news first: The world is not going to end. But something mysterious is happening. Something is not right. I will put before you all the facts and details and you can decide for yourself. I will put all the facts before you through biblical and scientific perspective and you can decide for yourself.

When I was doing all the research, I was wondering, "Why isn't the mainstream media reporting all these?" I was hearing small secret discussions here and there about these in some communities but there was no evidence to these things. So I decided to do extensive research on this and I couldn't believe myself on what I discovered. I was like," that's impossible. This cannot be happening." All of a sudden, everything started making sense. The "black lives matter" protest, the coronavirus, locust and all other mysterious happenings like "midday darkness" experienced in some parts of world started finally making sense.

If you too are wondering why all hell as been loosed all of a sudden on the Earth in 2020, then this book is for you. I have mentioned all the legitimate sources for you to double check on every single fact that I reveal to you. This is not science fiction. This is real life and we are living in mysterious times. It's okay if you do not know anything about the 10 plagues of Egypt. So grab a cup of coffee and join me in this journey of discovery of the 10 plagues of Egypt that has been unleashed upon the entire known world in 2020. Everything is based on true events.

ISBN: 9798663382274

For any queries, feel free to contact: **thetenplagues2020@gmail.com**

Table of Contents

The 10 Plagues of Egypt 1

Plague 1: The Nile turning to blood 9

Plague 2: Frogs 15

Plague 3: Plague of Mosquitoes/Gnats 20

Plague 4: The Plague of flies................................24

Plague 5: Pestilence 28

Plague 6: Boils..35

Plague 7: Hails and lightings 39

Plague 8: Locust 49

Plague 9: Plague of darkness................................55

Before the final plague: The wealth transfer 59

Plague 10: The final plague: the death of the firstborn 67

God of Israel VS the gods of Egypt 71

Disclaimer 89

The 10 Plagues of Egypt

AN INTRODUCTION

This all started 3 months ago in April. The Jews were celebrating the Passover and Christians all around the world were celebrating Easter. The entire world was on some form of lockdown. The great Coronavirus lockdown had just begun. A long time friend whom I haven't met for years calls me all of a sudden and says, "Hey, did you hear about it?" I was like, "hear about what?" Apparently, he heard some whispers in his community about how this year's Passover was different. I am not a Jew so for me it was not such a big deal. Few days later, I heard someone else talk about how after 3500 years, history is repeating itself. I too was wondering about the coronavirus and locusts plaguing the world. Intrigued, I decided to do some research about it.

I couldn't believe in what I discovered. So, I decided to do an extensive research on all the mysterious events happening all over the world. I also decided to study the Passover and the plagues of Egypt in detail. My friend was right. This year was indeed different. For those who do not know: Passover is an annual festival of the Jews celebrating the freedom from the slavery of the Egyptians. When I was doing my research in April, I didn't knew that two months later, entire world would be burning with "black lives matter" protest against racism. Egypt had enslaved the Israelites for 400 years and apparently the 400th anniversary of black slavery occurred on 2019. The first black slave entered US on 1619. So basically, blacks have been oppressed for 400 years just like the Israelites were oppressed for 400 years. It took 10 astounding plagues for the Pharaoh to free the Israelites. Maybe the history is indeed repeating itself after 3500 years.

In 2012, when it was said that the world was going to end, I knew that nothing was going to happen. At max, I anticipated an earthquake could have occurred in some random part of the Pacific. But things are different this time. For everything to make sense, we need to first understand the Passover and the 10 Plagues of Egypt.

Passover is the first festival that the Lord God of the Israelites commanded them to keep. It was on the night of Passover that the Lord unleashed the final plague on Egypt and delivered the Israelites from the slavery of Egypt. Jesus was crucified on the Passover and that makes it important for both Christians and Jews.

On the night of the first Passover, God was about to unleash the final plague on Egypt. Nine plagues had already brought Egypt to its knees. By this time, Egyptians had lost everything. They had lost half of their crops to hail and another half to locusts. They had lost all the fishes to the plague of Nile. They had lost most of their livestock to pestilence and the remaining to hailstones. They lost their health to boils. Plague after plague after plague had brought the biggest nation of that time to its knees to such an extent that Egyptians begged Pharaoh to let Israel go. But Pharaoh still refused to bow down. So, God was about to unleash the final plague on Egypt.

Exodus 10:7
Pharaoh's officials asked him, "How long must this man be a snare to us? Let the men go, so that they may worship the LORD their God. Don't you realize yet that Egypt is devastated?"

This was the night of 10th and final plague. Moses had commanded the Israelites to cover the doors of their houses with the blood of the lamb. Moses strictly commanded them to stay indoors. Those who are inside the houses covered by the blood would be spared and those who were outside would die.

Exodus 12: 22-23
*22Take a cluster of hyssop, dip it into the blood in the basin and brush the top and the two side posts of the door frame with some of the blood. **None of you***

shall go out of the door of his house until morning. *23When the LORD passes through to strike down the Egyptians, He will see the blood on the top and the two side posts and pass over the door; so He will not allow the destroyer to enter your houses and strike you down.*

Israel and Passover: The night of the final plague

The night of the first Passover, every Hebrew was inside the houses covered with the blood. They were witness to how the Lord had destroyed Egypt right before their eyes and that they couldn't afford to take the Lord lightly. So everyone was locked inside their house. After approximately 3500 years, this is the first time when the Jews were locked in their houses during this Passover. This has never happened in last 3500 years because for the last 2000 years, there was no Israel. After the Romans destroyed Jerusalem and the Temple in 70 AD, Jews were dispersed all throughout the Roman Empire: Europe and Asia. Since then, the majorities of the Jews settled all over Europe and were successful in their respective countries. Then came Hitler and killed 6 million Jews during the Holocaust. On May 14, 1948, Israel was born and the Jews from all over the world moved to Israel: The Promised Land.

After 2000 years, this is the very first time when the majority of Jews are together in one country and the first time in last 3500 years that majority of Jews are on lockdown during the Passover. This has never happened before.

On 19 March 2020, Prime Minister Benjamin Netanyahu of Israel declared a national state of emergency, tightening further on March 25 almost 2 weeks before the Passover. Passover this year started on April 8 and ended on April 16. So during this Passover in 2020, after 3500 years, the Jewish settlement not only in Israel but also all over the world was in lockdown. New York, the home to most number of Jews after Israel was on lockdown too.

This is not the first time that the world is suffering from a Plague and not the last time either. But this time it's different. All these events in the singular may not be significant but all of them happening at once all over the world might be a sign of something more to come. Before we discuss each of the plagues one by one, we need to understand the background of why God had to unleash the 10 plagues on Egypt. Let's discuss every single plague one by one and how it is manifesting itself in 2020.

Prelude to the plagues:

Around 3700 years ago, there was a great famine upon the entire known world. There was a huge scarcity of food in Mesopotamia but there was grain in Egypt thanks to the wisdom of its governor "Joseph". God gave a dream to Pharaoh about the famine that was about to come. So Egypt prepared for it. It stored all the excess grain for 7 years leading up to the famine that would last for 7 years. Joseph was a Hebrew. Due to the famine, Joseph settled his entire extended families in Egypt. Joseph was extremely powerful and great in Egypt. For 400 years, the Israelites lived in Egypt. They multiplied and were fruitful to so much extent that the Egyptians grew scared of them. This fear of the Jews made the Egyptians oppress them.

Exodus 1

Now Joseph and all his brothers and all that generation died, 7 but the Israelites were exceedingly fruitful; they multiplied greatly, increased in numbers and became so numerous that the land was filled with them.

8 Then a new king, to whom Joseph meant nothing, came to power in Egypt. 9 "Look," he said to his people, "the Israelites have become far too numerous for us. 10 Come, we must deal shrewdly with them or they will become even more numerous and, if war breaks out, will join our enemies, fight against us and leave the country."

11 So they put slave masters over them to oppress them with forced labour, and they built Pithom and Rameses as store cities for Pharaoh. 12 But the more they were oppressed, the more they multiplied and spread; so the Egyptians came to dread the Israelites 13 and worked them ruthlessly. 14 They made their lives bitter with harsh labour in brick and mortar and with all kinds of work in the fields; in all their harsh labour the Egyptians worked them ruthlessly.

The amazing thing is that all this was prophesied 400 years ago to Abraham by God. God told Abraham what would occur 400 years later in a vision.

Then the Lord said to him, "Know for certain that for four hundred years your descendants will be strangers in a country not their own and that they will be enslaved and mistreated there. 14 But I will punish the nation they serve as slaves, and afterwards they will come out with great possessions. 15 You, however, will go to your ancestors in peace and be buried at a good old age. 16 In the fourth generation, your descendants will come back here, for the sin of the Amorites has not yet reached its full measure."

This is exactly what happened. God foretold Abraham 400 years ago what was going to eventually happen in Egypt 8 generations later. Now 400 years later, Egypt had enslaved the Israelites. The Egyptians were bitter and harsh towards the Israelites and therefore under deep agony and pain, they cried out to God and God raised Moses to deliver them.

Moses presented himself to Pharaoh and demanded him to let the Israelites go. Pharaoh haughtily replied **"Who is the LORD that I should obey His voice and let Israel go? I do not know the LORD, and I will not let Israel go."**

This bluntness was the beginning of the plagues. Let's discuss all the plagues of Egypt one by one.

Plague 1: The Nile turning to blood

Exodus 7: 14-21

14 Then the Lord said to Moses, "Pharaoh's heart is stubborn and he still refuses to let the people go. 15 So go to Pharaoh in the morning as he goes down to the river. Stand on the bank of the Nile and meet him there. Be sure to take along the staff that turned into a snake. 16 Then announce to him, 'The Lord, the God of the Hebrews, has sent me to tell you, "Let my people go, so they can worship me in the wilderness." Until now, you have refused to listen to him. 17 So this is what the Lord says: "I will show you that I am the Lord." Look! I will strike the water of the Nile with this staff in my hand, and the river will turn to blood. 18 The fish in it will die, and the river will stink. The Egyptians will not be able to drink any water from the Nile.'"

19 Then the Lord said to Moses: "Tell Aaron, 'Take your staff and raise your hand over the waters of Egypt—all its rivers, canals, ponds, and all the reservoirs. Turn all the water to blood. Everywhere in Egypt, the water will turn to blood, even the water stored in wooden bowls and stone pots.'"

20 So Moses and Aaron did just as the Lord commanded them. As Pharaoh and all of his officials watched, Aaron raised his staff and struck the water of the Nile. Suddenly, the whole river turned to blood! 21 The fish in the river died, and the water became so foul that the Egyptians couldn't drink it. There was blood everywhere throughout the land of Egypt.

The first plague was the Nile River turning to blood. Not only river Nile but the lakes, ponds, water containers and pots all turned to blood.

The scientific explanation of water turning to bloody red is as follows:

Drought, heat, and increased demand for irrigation water shrinks the salty lakes and ponds. As the lake dries out, its salinity increases. The warm water's high salt concentration makes what's left of the lake a prime breeding ground for "Dunaliella" algae, which can turn the water blood-red.

"In the marine environment, Dunaliella salina appears green, however, in conditions of high salinity and light intensity, the micro-algae turns red due to the production of protective carotenoids in the cells: they produce pink-red pigments and when found in abundance, the pigments from these bacteria can turn super-salty water pink or red."

This is the scientific explanation of lakes or ponds turning to blood. But what happened in the Bible was not scientific, it was a plague. How do you explain the waters of containers in every home of Egypt turning red at once for 7 days? It was not only River Nile that turned blood but also lakes, ponds, irrigation channels and water stored in containers. Every drop of water in Egypt turned to blood. It doesn't say that the river turned into blood red but it says that the river turned to blood.

2020 corresponding to the plague of Nile:

The good news first: water has not turned to blood in 2020. Nothing similar has happened in 2020: rivers turning to blood. But rivers, lakes have started turning red (not blood) all over the world. Lakes and rivers turning to blood is a natural event that keeps on happening from time to time but this time something is different.

All of a sudden, rivers and lakes from all over the world have started turning red (not blood but red). Let's look at headlines of news articles below. You can search all of them on the internet as part of your research. All over the world, bodies of water are turning to blood-red for various reasons. Some are mysterious while others have a more logical explanation. Yet, for one reason or another, bodies of water all over the world are turning red.

1. Location: India

News: CNN
Time: June 12, 2020

A 50,000-year-old lake in India just turned pink and experts don't know exactly why

2. Location: Turkey
Time: April 26, 2020
News: dailysabah.com

Lake Meke in Turkey's central Konya province has dried up due to years of low rainfall and misuse of its water for agricultural purposes. The remaining puddles in the lakebed have turned red due to the microorganisms present.

3. Location: Russia
Time: April 24, 2020
News: Daily star. Co .UK

Water mysteriously turns red in 'blood river' as baffled officials probe incident
People were discussing the change of colour in Naro-Fominsk, Russia – which reportedly happened after an unknown spillage into the local Gvozdnya River

4. Location: Canada
Time: March 25, 2020
News: Daily star. Co. Uk

Canadian creek turns blood-red in creepy footage straight out of a horror film

Viewers claimed the footage was proof of biblical prophecies coming true, but there seems to be a more logical explanation.

5. Location: Mexican state of Zacatecas
News: Dailystar.co.uk
Time: 17 April 2020

Scientists baffled as lake turns red after 'lights in the sky' seen over village
Locals say they saw 'lights in the sky' and heard a strange 'roaring' sound before the lake mysteriously turned pink

6. Location: Newyork Lake Salubriya
News: Roserambles .org
Time: April 11, 2020

Another Body of Water Turns "Blood Red" New York State

7. Location: Israel
Time:16 May 2020
News: sun.co.uk

Israel river turns red with blood 'like the biblical plague of Egypt'

All these bodies of waters have turned red for different reasons. Some have turned red due to an oil spill, others due to bacteria and some due to pollution. But the point is the coincidence of all these turning red at one time.

These incidences are not unusual on their own and each of them has a very logical explanation .But the strange thing is the probability of rivers and lakes turning to red all over the world at almost same period of time. This is not common. Why 2020? Why didn't rivers all over the world turn to red in 2001 or 2014 or some other time?

During the plague of the Nile, thousands of fishes died. 3500 years later, something similar has happened. In 2019, millions of fishes died in Australia. Something similar happened again in 2020 due to the ashes of bush fire. Let's look at the headlines below:

phys.org, Jan, 2019
Million dead fish cause environmental stink in Australia

The Guardian, Jan, 2020
Hundreds of thousands of fish dead in NSW as bushfire ash washed into river

3500 years ago, one plague killed millions of fishes and today in 2019/2020 millions of fishes are dying for one reason or another.

Why are all the plagues: dead fishes, blood-red rivers and the Coronavirus manifesting themselves in 2020?

Plague 2: Frogs

The second plague was the plague of frogs. After the Nile River had turned to blood, Pharaoh still refused to let the Israelites go. So, God unleashed the second plague on Egypt.

Exodus 8

1 Then the Lord said to Moses, "Go to Pharaoh and say to him, 'This is what the Lord says: Let my people go, so that they may worship me. 2 If you refuse to let them go, I will send a plague of frogs on your whole country. 3 The Nile will teem with frogs. They will come up into your palace and your bedroom and onto your bed, into the houses of your officials and on your people, and into your ovens and kneading troughs. 4 The frogs will come upon you and your people and all your officials.'"

5 Then the Lord said to Moses, "Tell Aaron, 'Stretch out your hand with your staff over the streams and canals and ponds, and make frogs come upon the land of Egypt.'"

6 So Aaron stretched out his hand over the waters of Egypt, and the frogs came up and covered the land.

Entire Egypt was covered with frogs. Frogs were considered sacred in ancient Egypt. They were considered deity because they lived in both land and water. Killing them was punishable by death. Now imagine, frogs covering everything but you cannot kill them because you worship them. The frogs were in the bedroom, bathroom, living room and all over the floor. The Egyptian magician by their secret magic also could bring the frog. But they couldn't take it away. So, fed up with frogs Pharaoh called Moses and requested him to make the frogs go away. Moses prayed to God and all the millions of frogs died. The Egyptians collected the dead frogs that they viewed so sacred.

But the magicians did the same things by their secret arts; they also made frogs come upon the land of Egypt.

8 Pharaoh summoned Moses and Aaron and said, "Pray to the Lord to take the frogs away from me and my people, and I will let your people go to offer sacrifices to the Lord."

9 Moses said to Pharaoh, "I leave to you the honour of setting the time for me to pray for you and your officials and your people that you and your houses may be rid of the frogs, except for those that remain in the Nile."

10 "Tomorrow," Pharaoh said.

Moses replied, "It will be as you say, so that you may know there is no one like the Lord our God. 11 The frogs will leave you and your houses, your officials and your people; they will remain only in the Nile."

12 After Moses and Aaron left Pharaoh, Moses cried out to the Lord about the frogs he had brought on Pharaoh. 13 And the Lord did what Moses asked. The frogs died in the houses, in the courtyards and in the fields. 14 They were piled into heaps, and the land reeked of them. 15 But when Pharaoh saw that there was a relief, he hardened his heart and would not listen to Moses and Aaron, just as the Lord had said

2020 corresponding to the plague of the frogs:

Time: June 11, 2020
Location: Florida, USA
News: USA today

Florida tells residents to humanely kill these invasive, toxic toads that are lethal to pets

WP TV:

Heat, rain creating a breeding ground for toxic toads, iguanas in South Florida

We had a lot last year. We're seeing, even more, this year," said the owner of Toad Busters, a poisonous toad removal company.
Wildlife experts are issuing a new warning after an explosion of toxic toads.

Florida had a major outbreak of poisonous toads last year in 2019. This year it's worst. Although Florida's climate is more favorable to frogs and it's not a "new thing" in Florida, the fact that major outbreak of frogs in 2019-2020 has coincided with Covid-19 might be little more than coincidence.

This is the news headlines from 2019:

Time .com, March 2019

Poisonous Toads Are Swarming This Florida Town
Thousands of toxic toads have invaded a Florida suburb, worrying pet-owners and parents, reports CBS News.
Bufo toads, also known as cane toads, have come out in droves in Palm Beach Gardens on Florida's East Coast. "You can't even walk through the grass without stepping on one; they're covering people's driveway," one homeowner told CBS Miami.

The Florida frog epidemic was not making sense in 2019 but now putting every dot together, we are seeing a pattern. Maybe, the frog plague in itself didn't make sense in 2019 but it makes a lot of sense now. I always wondered why God killed millions of frogs. I mean He could have sent them back to Nile. But it was an attack on "the deity" of the Egyptians that they viewed so sacred. Like millions of frogs died that day 3500 years ago, millions of frogs are dying today. Look at the headlines from March, 2019:

Newyork Times, March 2019
The Plague Killing Frogs Everywhere Is Far Worse Than Scientists Thought
As a threat to wildlife, an amphibian fungus has become "the most deadly pathogen known to science."

March, 2019 National Geographic
Amphibian 'apocalypse' caused by most destructive pathogen

Thousands of species of frogs dying in 2019 and the coronavirus manifesting itself in 2019 might not just be a coincidence. 3500 years ago, hundreds of thousands of frogs died and today thousands of them are dying. Can this be a coincidence?

Plague 3: Plague of Mosquitoes/Gnats

The Plague of Gnats
Exodus 8:16-19
[16]Then the Lord said to Moses, Say to Aaron, Stretch out your rod and strike the dust of the ground, that it may become biting gnats or mosquitoes throughout all the land of Egypt.

[17]And they did so; Aaron stretched out his hand with his rod and struck the dust of the earth, and there came biting gnats or mosquitoes on man and beast; all the dust of the land became biting gnats or mosquitoes throughout all the land of Egypt.

[18]The magicians tried by their enchantments and secret arts to bring forth gnats or mosquitoes, but they could not, and there were gnats or mosquitoes on man and beast.

[19]Then the magicians said to Pharaoh, This is the finger of God! But Pharaoh's heart was hardened and strong and he would not listen to them, just as the Lord had said.

There is confusion around the exact definition of gnats. Some say its mosquitoes and others say it's lice. Few

Jewish commentators and some historians like Josephus consider it as lice while everyone else considers it as mosquitoes. Lice make little sense because the wisest and predominant members of society chose to simply shave their entire bodies. The majority of scholars and historians favour mosquitoes. The amplified Bible mentions mosquitoes clearly.

Egypt was a desert and it was normal to have sand particles everywhere: in the land, in air and inside houses. We can just imagine how big this plague was because Egypt had a lot of dusts and these dusts changed into mosquitoes. Only God can create something out of dust.

The magicians of Egypt surrendered because only God can give life and turn dust to life. This plague was given without warning because Pharaoh broke his promise that he made to Moses after the plague of frogs to let the Israelites go.

2020 corresponding plague of Mosquitoes/ Gnats:

Minnesota CBS local March 14, 2020
Are This Year's Gnats Worse Than In The Past?

Star Tribune Minnesota, USA May 15, 2020
Now what? Gnats? Black fly invasion torments Twin Cities

Just when you thought you could find relief outdoors amid a global pandemic, swarms of aggressive black flies have emerged to ravage the Twin Cities.
"They're just awful," said a local resident, who was swarmed and bitten within minutes of stepping outside her Plymouth home, where, like most Minnesotans, she's hunkered down during the state stay-at-home orders to fight COVID-19.

LA Times May 12, 2020
Coronavirus overshadows another dangerous viral outbreak: Dengue

To those who do not know, dengue and other mosquito-related diseases had been an epidemic in 2019 in South Asia and Southeast Asia popularly known as the 2019–2020 dengue fever epidemic. The 2019–2020 dengue fever epidemic occurred in several countries of Asia, including the Philippines, Malaysia, Vietnam, and Bangladesh, Nepal Pakistan, Thailand, Singapore, and Laos.

The world is battling not only the coronavirus but also the dengue epidemic caused by mosquitoes. Not just Asia, but major outbreaks of mosquito-related illnesses are seen all over the world. Malaria, dengue, Zika virus, yellow fever all are caused by mosquitoes.

Al Jazeera 12 May 2020
Dengue kills too': Latin America faces two epidemics at once

Experts expect 2020 to be marked by high rates of dengue, which can fill ICUs even absent the pressures of coronavirus.

May 24, 2020, vaxbeforetravel.com
Yellow Fever Outbreaks Reported in Africa
Pre-travel yellow fever vaccination recommended when visiting endemic areas in Africa and South America

CGTN April 23, 2020
Ethiopia at risk of Yellow Fever outbreak, WHO says

The East African Tuesday, April 14 2020
WHO declares Yellow fever outbreak in South Sudan

21 April 2020, The Guardian
Zimbabwe faces malaria outbreak as it locks down to counter coronavirus

Medical express 23 April 2020
WHO warns malaria deaths could double during virus pandemic

So basically the third plague is already here. Maybe it is hidden or not getting enough media attention but it is here. The world is battling not only coronavirus but mosquitoes related illnesses.

Plague 4: The Plague of flies

The Plague of Flies

20 Then the Lord said to Moses, "Get up early in the morning and confront Pharaoh as he goes to the river and say to him, 'This is what the Lord says: Let my people go, so that they may worship me. 21 If you do not let my people go, I will send swarms of flies on you and your officials, on your people and into your houses. The houses of the Egyptians will be full of flies; even the ground will be covered with them.

22 "'But on that day I will deal differently with the land of Goshen, where my people live; no swarms of flies will be there so that you will know that I, the Lord, am in this land. 23 I will make a distinction between my people and your people. This sign will occur tomorrow.'"

24 And the Lord did this. Dense swarms of flies poured into Pharaoh's palace and into the houses of his officials; throughout Egypt, the land was ruined by the flies.

The fourth plague is debated. The actual Hebrew word used for flies is **"arov"**. Some debate it to be a swarm of insects and others debate it to be wild animals. Wild animals make little sense because "dense swarms of flies poured into Pharaoh Palace and houses of his official" cannot be associated with them. The passage just doesn't make sense with the swarm of wild animals. If a gang of wild animals tried entering the Palace, they would have been killed by the Egyptian army using arrows and swords. The amplified Bible gives a more accurate translation. The exact name of the insect is not given but it has to be a swarm of insects: probably millions of insects.

The amplified Bible is more descriptive:

Exodus 8:21
[21]Else, if you will not let My people go, behold, I will send swarms **[of bloodsucking gadflies]** upon you, your servants, and your people, and into your houses; and the houses of the Egyptians shall be full of swarms [of bloodsucking gadflies], and also the ground on which they stand.

With the fourth Egyptian plague, which consisted of flies, begins the great miracle of separation or differentiation. This time, however, only the Egyptians are affected by the judgement or plague, and the children of Israel remained unscratched. This wonder also moves the Egyptian plagues to a different level, adding destruction as well as discomfort to the consequence of their decisions.

2020 corresponding to the plague of flies:

1. Location: London, UK

18 May 2020 Walesonline.co.uk
Warning over bloodsucking Blandford flies invading UK - here's what to do if you've been bitten
The nasty bugs can cause serious and painful reactions, including swelling in the groin, a fever and blistering

2. Location: Thailand

April 30, 2020, nationthailand.com
Symptoms of African horse sickness aired as Thailand suffers first-ever outbreak

*The disease was first found in Nakhon Ratchasima but has now spread via **mosquitoes, gnats and gadflies** to other parts of the country, killing hundreds of horses, as well as zebras, camels, donkeys and mules.*

3. Location: UK

April 11, 2020, itv.com
Coronavirus lockdown 'nightmare' as flies swarm homes in Avonmouth

Families cooped up inside during the coronavirus lockdown have been plagued by swarms of flies which have turned a Bristol suburb into a 'double nightmare'.

4. Location: Texas, USA

March 30, 2020 messenger news
Outbreak of Black Flies in East Texas

They can be a real problem in humans, domestic animals, horses, cattle, poultry, sheep, goats, dogs and deer. Back flies are transmitters of pathogens (nematodes, protozoans and viruses) that can cause disease. Black fly females have very painful bites and can exhibit nuisance swarms. Large numbers of black flies can cause bird, poultry and livestock death.

5. Location: Louisiana, USA

Apr 13, 2020 location: Louisiana; *Wbrz.com*
Outbreak of biting gnats, black flies in Baton Rouge

Plague 5: Pestilence

Exodus 9:1-7

[1]THEN THE Lord said to Moses, Go to Pharaoh and tell him, Thus says the Lord God of the Hebrews: Let My people go, that they may serve Me.
[2]If you refuse to let them go and still hold them,
[3]Behold, the hand of the Lord [will fall] upon your livestock which are out in the field, upon the horses, the donkeys, the camels, the herds and the flocks; there shall be a very severe plague.
[4]But the Lord shall make a distinction between the livestock of Israel and the livestock of Egypt, and nothing shall die of all that belongs to the Israelites.
[5]And the Lord set a time, saying, Tomorrow the Lord will do this thing in the land.
[6]And the Lord did that the next day and all [kinds of] the livestock of Egypt died, but of the livestock of the Israelites, not one died.
[7]Pharaoh sent to find out, and behold, there was not one of the cattle of the Israelites dead. But the heart of Pharaoh was hardened [his mind was set and he did not let the people go].

Plague number 5 was the pestilence upon the livestock. Livestock was the lifeline of the Egyptian economy. They were used in irrigation, army, and transportation and for dairy products. Some livestock like cows and bulls were considered sacred in ancient Egypt. This plague was a direct hit on them. This plague hit Egypt on the core of its economy.

But God again made a distinction between Israel and Egypt. All kinds of animals that belong to the Egyptians died but not one of the livestock that belonged to Israelis died. It was such an economic disaster and the pestilence was so widespread that Pharaoh couldn't believe that not one of the animals of the Israelites died. He sent his men to check on it and it was reported to Pharaoh that not one was dead among the Israelites. However, not all livestock died in this plague. Some remained for the future plagues.

2020 corresponding to the plague of pestilence upon livestock:

Horses:

Bangkok Post 18 MAY 2020
Horse deaths lead to race against time
Deadly plague costing millions blamed on zebras imported from Africa. After nearly two months, the first-ever outbreak of African Horse Sickness (AHS) in Thailand has wiped out 539 horses

Chickens:

New York Times April 28, 2020
Nearly 2 Million Chickens Killed as Poultry Workers Are Sidelined

March 11 2020 news18.com
Location: India
Karnataka Poultry Farmer Buries Alive 6,000 Chickens in Mass Grave as Coronavirus Impacts Sale

The observers
Iranian poultry farmers bury thousands of chicks alive as Covid-19 hits demand

Feb 2020
CNBC
Hundreds of millions of chickens at risk of being wiped out with much of China locked down due to virus

Similar cases have been seen all over the world: in China, Nepal, Iran, Southeast Asia. Poultry farmers all over the world had to kill millions of chickens because of the Coronavirus Pandemic. The rumors that coronavirus can spread through chicken meat caused a slump in demand. With thousands of chickens on the farm and no sales at all, the cost of food for the chicken was not sustainable for the business. Businesses all over the world have killed millions of chickens.

We discussed above the effect of coronavirus on chicken. But that's not all. Look at the headlines below:

May 2020, wattagnet.com
Further avian flu outbreaks confirmed in Hungarian poultry
Avian flu losses rise sharply in Hungary.
Signs of the disease were observed on 61 Hungarian farms and in two backyards flocks between April 14 and May 2

May 2020, wattagnet.com
Highly pathogenic avian flu returns to Iraq
More than 21,700 birds die at Iraqi farm

Feb 2020
Authorities Try To Contain Bird Flu Outbreak in Southern Bulgaria

Vax before travel; May 2020
Bird-Flu Outbreak Confirmed in China

All over the world, there are mini outbreaks of bird flu. It keeps on happening from time to time. It's not something new. In 2015, during the outbreak of avian flu, millions of chickens were slaughtered. The pestilence mentioned in the 5th plague must be a similar disease.

Swine:

Swine flu and African swine fever are threatening the lives of millions of pigs all over the world. Poland, Africa, China, India and many others are battling with ASF.

ASF kills almost 100% of the animals it infects, and despite being in circulation for nearly 100 years, there is still no vaccine.

ASF had been a problem for many years, but when it reached China in autumn 2018 the disease exploded and the following year saw huge numbers of deaths. The official count was of around 1.1 million pigs culled in the year after that according to the UN Food and Agriculture Organization (FAO).

Unofficially, however, China's numbers were probably closer to 200 million or more pigs culled, slaughtered early or lost to the disease in the first year of the outbreak. According to estimation, at least 40% of the country's 360 million pig population could have been lost.

Al Jazeera Feb 2020

Swine fever: 'Double punch' for countries facing COVID-19 threat

Disease is harmless to humans but has wiped out 60 percent of China's swine industry and a quarter of global supply

May 2020, the Guardian

Unstoppable': African swine fever deaths to eclipse record 2019 toll

With world's attention on Covid-19, warnings that lack of measures to contain pandemic could lead to culling of record number of pigs

June 10, BBC

African swine fever 'decimating' Nigerian pigs

Some 300,000 pigs have been killed

The diplomat, May 2020

India's Northeast Hit By the African Swine Fever

More than 14,000 pigs have died in Assam alone.

Cattles are being killed everywhere. Some die due to diseases. Others are killed due to the market slump caused by the coronavirus. 3500 years ago, the plague killed thousands on livestock and today one plague or another is killing thousands of livestock. Can all of this be just a mere coincidence? Yes, we have bird flu outbreak from time to time, yes we have swine flu outbreak from time to time but all the outbreaks at one time cannot be just a coincidence. Just this month (June 2020), there has been a rare resurgence of donkey diseases. Look at the headlines below:

June 5, 2020 mirage news

A parasitic disease affecting donkeys is detected in the UK for the first time

June 2020 horsetalk.co.nz

Mysterious parasitic disease of equines confirmed in donkeys in Britain

All of this cannot be a mere coincidence. All the resurgence of viruses all over the world cannot be a coincidence.

Plague 6: Boils

Exodus 9:8-11

[8]The Lord said to Moses and Aaron, Take handfuls of ashes or soot from the brick kiln and let Moses sprinkle them toward the heavens in the sight of Pharaoh.

[9]And it shall become small dust over all the land of Egypt, and become boils breaking out in sores on man and beast in all the land [occupied by the Egyptians].

[10]So they took ashes or soot of the kiln and stood before Pharaoh, and Moses threw them toward the sky, and it became boils erupting in sores on man and beast.

[11]And the magicians could not stand before Moses because of their boils; for the boils were on the magicians and all the Egyptians.

Unannounced the sixth Egyptian plague is given, for the first time, directly attacking the Egyptian people themselves. The severity of the judgment of God has now become personal, as it is felt by the people themselves.

Something is interesting about this plague. Moses took ash from the furnace and threw them towards the heavens. We do not know exactly what kind of furnace was this. Most probably, this should be a brick furnace that denotes the 400-year oppression of the Israelites from the hands of the Egyptians. This makes sense for the plague to be personal. This plague was personal. The people of Egypt, every single one of them was being judged for being harsh to Israelites and oppressing them for 400 years. This was justice because every day they were troubled and oppressed by the Egyptians. It was time people of Egypt were punished for their wrongdoing against the Israelites. But not only that, this plague was a warning that the LORD God of Israel could not only unleash plagues upon their livestock and environment but also themselves. They finally felt the pain of the plagues. This was also a warning that if the LORD could bring disease to their body, he could also kill them. This was important so that when the final plague of the death of firstborn was manifested later, at least some of them would have repented.

There is another side to this story. There was an Egyptian custom of scattering to the winds ashes of victims offered to Egyptian god Seth: the god of serpents, black magic and spells. He was a god of destruction. Humans were sacrificed to him and their ashes were thrown into the wind as blessings upon the Egyptians. When Moses took ash (most probably) from the brick furnace and threw it upon the heavens, the ashes that were a symbol of blessings brought a plague upon the Egyptians as the judgement for the sins of human sacrifice. An ash that was a symbol for their blessings was now a curse for them.

2020 corresponding to the plague of boils:

The good news first: We don't have a boils outbreak at the present. The sixth plague was an acute epidemic skin disease, though probably not deadly, characterized by boils. It was a kind of skin disease that anyone could see. It was upon humans and animals. We don't know exactly what these boils were and their proper medical designation but we do know it was skin related. It should be most probably large and tiny red spots all over the body. The Coronavirus has something similar that is very mysterious to doctors.

2 May 2020 BBC
Coronavirus: 'COVID toe' and other rashes puzzle doctors

Five rashes, including COVID toe, are affecting some hospital patients diagnosed with Covid-19, a small study by Spanish doctors has found.

The rashes tended to appear in younger people and lasted several days. It is not uncommon for a rash to be a symptom of a virus, such as the spots that indicate chickenpox. But the researchers said they were surprised to see so many varieties of rash with Covid-19. Rashes are not currently included in the list of symptoms of the illness.

Live science May 2020

More than 'COVID toes': Numerous reports of skin rashes tied to COVID-19

Numerous reports of skin rashes in patients with COVID-19 are cropping up around the world.

*The rashes can take many forms — some appear as **tiny red spots**, while others appear as **larger flat or raised lesions.** Some have a hive-like appearance, while others look like frostbitten toes.*
It's unclear whether the skin lesions we see in COVID are actually a direct manifestation of the virus" in the skin, or whether they are a "reaction pattern" due to a generally ramped-up immune system

We do not know what the boils were during the sixth plague but we do know it was something skin related and something visible. What are boils? Are they not red spots like some coronavirus patients are experiencing? Large skin lesions are similar: they are red spots that are clearly visible just as boils. Now rashes and boils are different but both of them are skin related and therefore visible.

Is it just a coincidence that the Coronavirus is having these symptoms in some patients? There have been so many other virus outbreaks but why weren't these skin symptoms present in those epidemics? Why are the boils like skin-related issues manifesting themselves during the 2020 coronavirus pandemic?

Plague 7: Hails and lightings

Exodus 9:13-26
[13]Then the Lord said to Moses, Rise up early in the morning and stand before Pharaoh and say to him, Thus says the Lord, the God of the Hebrews, Let My people go, that they may serve Me.

[14]For this time I will send all My plagues upon your heart and upon your servants and your people, that you may recognize and know that there is none like Me in all the earth.

[15]For by now I could have put forth My hand and have struck you and your people with pestilence, and you would have been cut off from the earth.

[16]But for this very purpose have I let you live, that I might show you My power, and that My name may be declared throughout all the earth.

[17]Since you are still exalting yourself [in haughty defiance] against My people by not letting them go,

[18]Behold, tomorrow about this time I will cause it to rain a very heavy and dreadful fall of hail, such as has not been in Egypt from its founding until now.

[19]Send therefore now and gather your cattle in hastily, and all that you have in the field; for every man and beast that is in the field and is not brought home shall be struck by the hail and shall die.

[20]Then he who feared the word of the Lord among the servants of Pharaoh made his servants and his livestock flee into the houses and shelters.

[21]And he who ignored the word of the Lord left his servants and his livestock in the field.

[22]The Lord said to Moses, Stretch forth your hand toward the heavens, that there may be hail in all the land of Egypt, upon man and beast, and upon all the vegetation of the field, throughout the land of Egypt.

[23]Then Moses stretched forth his rod toward the heavens, and the Lord sent thunder and hail, and fire (lightning) ran down to and along the ground, and the Lord rained hail upon the land of Egypt.

[24]So there was hail and fire flashing continually in the midst of the weighty hail, such as had not been in all the land of Egypt since it became a nation.

[25]The hail struck down throughout all the land of Egypt everything that was in the field, both man and beast; and the hail beat down all the vegetation of the field and shattered every tree of the field.

[26]Only in the land of Goshen, where the Israelites were, was there no hail.

Egypt is a desert country. The country still receives hardly any significant rain. Egypt was completely dependent on the Nile for all its irrigation. Irrigation canals were made to bring the water from the Nile into the fields. The Egyptians were not habitual to heavy thunderstorms.

But this was not a thunderstorm, this was a plague. We can understand the intensity of the plague by the fact that everything that was outside died: man and beast. We are experiencing something similar right now in 2020. This was the first time a warning was given to Egyptians to lock themselves up with their remaining livestock and not to step out of the house. God in his mercy gave a warning to the Egyptians to save their lives. All the Egyptians who had enough of the plagues humbled themselves before the Lord and took heed to his warning and remained in their house.

Exodus 9:20
Then he who feared the word of the Lord among the servants of Pharaoh made his servants and his livestock flee into the houses and shelters.

The remaining who believed that there was no way that Egypt which was a desert would receive hail and thunder of that proportion that could kill men and livestock remained outside and were killed. Rock sized hailstones were unheard of. Hails are generally very small in size and definitely not fatal. By now, they should have taken the plagues seriously but it's awful to see how haughty they had been even after all these plagues. They were mistaken to consider the hail and thunderstorms as normal because this was not a normal rain, this was a plague.

This was a total economic disaster for Egypt. Egyptians were killed. Livestock were killed. Flax and barley were ripe for harvest but they were destroyed. Only wheat was not destroyed because it had not grown yet. This affected the very food that Egyptians ate. Famine was imminent. The little that was left would be destroyed in the next plague.

Exodus 9:27-34
*[27]And Pharaoh sent for Moses and Aaron, and said to them, **I have sinned this time; the Lord is in the right and I and my people are in the wrong.***

*[28]Entreat the Lord, for there has been **enough of these mighty thunderings** and hail [these voices of God]; I will let you go; you shall stay here no longer.*

[29]Moses said to him, As soon as I leave the city, I will stretch out my hands to the Lord; the thunder shall cease, neither shall there be any more hail, that you may know that the earth is the Lord's.

[30]But as for you and your servants, I know that you do not yet [reverently] fear the Lord God.

[31]The flax and the barley were smitten and ruined, for the barley was in the ear and the flax in bloom.

[32]But the wheat and spelt [another wheat] were not smitten, for they ripen late and were not grown up yet.

[33]So Moses left the city and Pharaoh, and stretched forth his hands to the Lord; and the thunder and hail ceased, and rain was no longer poured upon the earth.

[34]But when Pharaoh saw that the rain, the hail, and the thunder had ceased, he sinned yet more, and toughened and stiffened his hard heart, he and his servants.

Looks like Pharaoh never learned a lesson. The hailstones destroyed not only men and cattle on the fields but also their crops having a huge economic impact on Egypt.

2020 corresponding to the plague of hail:

Isn't it amazing that the warning was given to the Egyptians to stay indoors just like the warnings given by governments all around the world for us to stay indoors? The warning was simple: stay indoors and live or stay outside and die. People all over the world are experiencing something similar in 2020. Let's act like the wise servants of Pharaoh not like the foolish ones.

We all know-how in recent years severe hail storms have become a norm. During hail storms, we expect a normal size of hailstones. But the world is experiencing something different right now.

All the news below is from 2020.

On 13, May 2020, Mexico received a heavy rain and hail storm. The stones were so big it became viral on the internet. Some of the stones were shaped like coronavirus, so it led to widespread media coverage. Recently, the same things are being experienced all over the world. I bet a lot of us have experienced huge hailstones recently or maybe are going to experience soon. On may 23, 2020. Something similar happened in Petrolia,Texas.

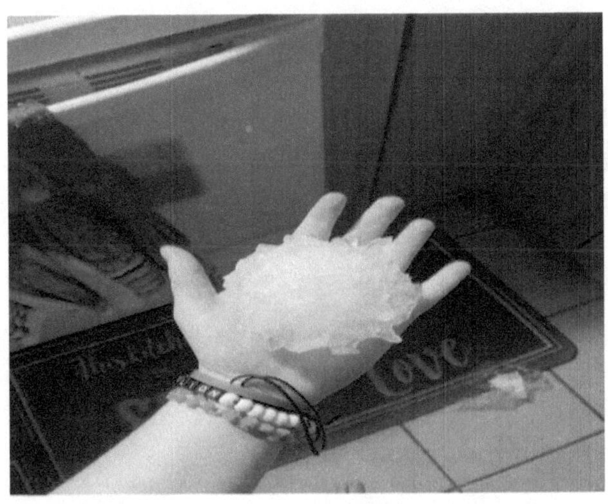

Not just North America, something similar is experienced all over the world. On 19, April 2020 something similar happened in the Himalayan country of Nepal:

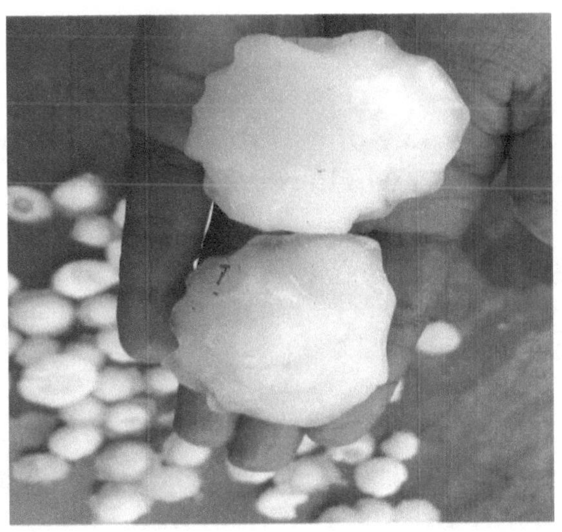

Look at this year's news articles below:

Asia:
April 23, 2020 watchers news
Intense hailstorm destroys hundreds of homes in Nagaland, India

Heavy rains accompanied by strong winds and large hail, up to 5 cm (2 inches) in diameter, lashed several villages in the district of Kiphire in Nagaland, northeast India, on April 21, 2020, damaging or destroying more than 500 homes.

Europe:
June 17, 2020, watchers news
Massive hailstorm hits northeastern Spain, expected to drastically affect European stone fruit season

South America:
May 2, 2020, CNN
Hailstone the size of a football in Argentina may have smashed a world record

Australia:
This is the news after the huge hailstone on 21 January 2020 in Australia.

The Washington Post
Plagues of extreme weather descend on Australia, with destructive hail, dust storms and flooding

The guardian:

Huge hail batters Canberra as severe thunderstorms hit south-eastern Australia

ABC News:

What has made the hail so bad over the past few days?

Africa:
March 31, 2020

Intense hailstorm hits Middelburg, South Africa
An intense hailstorm hit the town of Middelburg in Mpumalanga, South Africa, on March 27, 2020, causing extensive damage. The incident was dubbed a "disaster within a disaster" as it came on the same day the country started its three-week coronavirus lockdown.

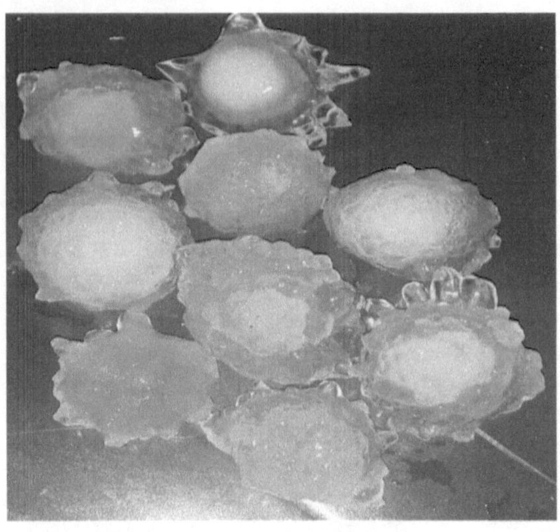

We have covered every continent in the world. Hailstones are nothing new but hailstones of the size of rock are not something that we see every day. We all have experienced how the hailstones are getting more and more dangerous with time. I don't recall watching such gigantic hailstones one or two decades ago.

When the entire world is battling coronavirus, hailstones have become another disaster. It has become a disaster within a disaster.

Plague 8: Locust

Exodus 10:3-7
[3]So Moses and Aaron went to Pharaoh, and said to him, Thus says the Lord, the God of the Hebrews, How long will you refuse to humble yourself before Me? Let My people go, that they may serve Me.

[4]For if you refuse to let My people go, behold, tomorrow I will bring locusts into your country.

*[5]And they shall cover the land so that one cannot see the ground, and they shall eat the remainder of what escaped and is left to you from the hail, and **they shall eat every tree of yours that grows in the field;***

*[6]The locusts shall fill your houses and those of all your servants and of all the Egyptians, as **neither your fathers nor your fathers' fathers have seen from their birth until this day.** Then Moses departed from Pharaoh.*

*[7]And Pharaoh's servants said to him, How long shall this man be a snare to us? **Let the men go, that they may serve the Lord their God; do you not yet understand and know that Egypt is destroyed?***

By this time, Egypt was destroyed. The people have had enough of the plagues. They were tired yet Pharaoh and some of his servants refused to humble themselves before God.

From an economic perspective, Egypt was destroyed. By now :

The first plague of the "Nile turning to blood" had destroyed all fishes.

The fourth plague of blood-sucking insects and the fifth plague of pestilence destroyed a majority of their livestock. The remaining was destroyed by hailstones. The little livestock remained of those Egyptians who humbled themselves before the Lord and took heed of His warning. There was no way a domestic animal and cattle could survive both the plagues: hailstones and pestilence. Egyptians had little livestock left.

The hailstones also destroyed barley and flax which comprised a significant portion of their crops. The remainder was going to be destroyed by the locusts. Agriculture was over. Their economy was over. The economy of Egypt was completely dependent on fishes, livestock and crops and all of them were completely destroyed. Locusts eat everything that is green. The trees that were remaining after the hailstones were destroyed by the locust. All the fruits were destroyed. All the vegetation was destroyed. The wheat that was yet to grow was eaten by the locust. The economy of

Egypt was finished. Even if the Lord stopped the plagues here, a lot of Egyptians would have died out of hunger. The remaining livestock (if any remained) would die of hunger because locusts ate everything. There was no food left for the livestock.

A Desert Locust adult can consume roughly its own weight in fresh food per day that is about two grams every day. A 1 square kilometers size swarm contains about 40 million locusts, which eat the same amount of food in one day as about 35,000 people.

Exodus 10:12-20
*[12]Then the Lord said to Moses, Stretch out your hand over the land of Egypt for the **locusts, that they may come upon the land of Egypt and eat all the vegetation of the land, all that the hail has left.***

[13]And Moses stretched forth his rod over the land of Egypt, and the Lord brought an east wind upon the land all that day and all that night; when it was morning, the east wind brought the locusts.

*[14]And the locusts came up over all the land of Egypt and settled down on the whole country of Egypt, a very dreadful mass of them; **never before were there such locusts as these, nor will there ever be again.***

*[15]**For they covered the whole land, so that the ground was darkened, and they ate every bit of***

vegetation of the land and all the fruit of the trees which the hail had left; there remained not a green thing of the trees or the plants of the field in all the land of Egypt.

[16]Then Pharaoh sent for Moses and Aaron in haste. He said, I have sinned against the Lord your God and you.

[17]Now, therefore, forgive my sin, I pray you, only this once, and entreat the Lord your God only that He may remove from me this [plague of] death.

[18]Then Moses left Pharaoh and entreated the Lord.

[19]And the Lord turned a violent west wind, which lifted the locusts and drove them into the Red Sea; not one locust remained in all the country of Egypt.

[20]But the Lord made Pharaoh's heart more strong and obstinate, and he would not let the Israelites go.

2020 corresponding to the plague of locusts:

This is not breaking news. We all know about the havoc that the huge swarms of locust have had upon East Africa, the Middle East and South Asia. Biblical proportions of locust are bringing destruction upon more than two dozen countries all around the world. These tiny creatures have brought big and powerful nations to its knees rendering them helpless. These nations have tried everything they can yet seem to be powerless against these billions of locusts.

Although locusts are nothing new, we didn't have a major outbreak of this proportion in many decades. Just look at this statement from the UN agency:

"In Kenya, it's the worst outbreak they've had to face in the last 70 years," says Keith Cressman, the U.N. Food and Agriculture Organization's senior locust forecasting officer. "In India or Pakistan, it's probably the worst they've had to face in the last quarter of a century."

The swarms consist of tens of billions of flying grasshoppers that range anywhere from a square third of a mile to 100 square miles or more, with 40 million to 80 million locusts packed in half a square mile. They bulldoze pasturelands in dark clouds the size of football fields and small cities. In northern Kenya, one swarm was reported to be 24 times bigger than the city of Paris.

Locusts are ravenous eaters. An adult desert locust that weighs about 2 grams can consume roughly its own weight daily. A small swarm (1 square kilometer) can be made up of 80 million locusts and can consume the same amount of food in one day as 35,000 people, while a large swarm can eat up to 1.8 million metric tons of green vegetation, equivalent to food enough to feed 81 million people. Locusts breed very fast and— a single female locust can lay egg pods containing anywhere from 80- 150 eggs. They can cause 50 to 80% of crops to be destroyed, depending on the time of the year. This year Monsoon in Asia might cause heavy breeding of locusts in Asia while there is already the second wave of locust in East Africa.

The forecast indicates that more than 25 million people in the East Africa region will face acute food insecurity in the latter half of the year. An additional 17 million people in Yemen are already affected. Here is a news article from The Guardian:

April 2020
The Guardian
Second wave of locusts in east Africa said to be 20 times worse

We thought we were dealing with the first and second wave of only the coronavirus but looks like locust are also attacking in waves.

Plague 9: Plague of darkness

Exodus 10:21-23

[21]And the Lord said to Moses, Stretch out your hand toward the heavens, that there may be darkness over the land of Egypt, a darkness which may be felt.

[22]So Moses stretched out his hand toward the sky, and for three days a thick darkness was all over the land of Egypt.

*[23]**The Egyptians could not see one another, nor did anyone rise from his place for three days;** but all the Israelites had natural light in their dwellings.*

This was a plague. This darkness was not the mere absence of light. If it were, it could have easily been put away by candles and sunrise but the darkness was there for 3 days. Egypt was a country with 365 days of light and scourging sun. They had never lived with darkness more than a couple of hours at night. Imagine, when the sky turned dark, people hoped that, "Tomorrow when the sun rises, we will have light again." But the next day, they don't see a ray of light. It's 5 am and there is no sunrise. They hope the sun will rise by 6 am.

But the sun doesn't rise upon them. Imagine the horror that would be on their mind when the sun didn't rise on Egypt the next day. This is not to say that the sun didn't rise literally all over the world but the darkness was so thick that not even a ray of light entered Egypt. Entire Egypt should have been in absolute horror because they must have assumed that their most powerful god, Ra is dead. This partially explains why they didn't move from one place to another. For 3 days, there was no light and absolute darkness that they could feel. We have never experienced such a thing so probably we cannot understand their pain but we have to understand that this was a plague and the judgement of Jehovah on their most powerful god: Ra. To an Egyptian mind, the sun god Ra: the most powerful god in Egypt would have been assumed to be dead. This explains why Pharaoh immediately allowed Moses and the Israelites to leave Egypt but demanded their livestock stay in Egypt because Egypt has little left due to the plague. But this was not acceptable to Moses.

We have to understand the significance of this plague. This was the sign that the LORD had defeated the most powerful sun god of Egypt. This made Moses extremely great in Egypt.

Exodus 11:3
*[3]And the Lord gave the people favour in the sight of the Egyptians. Moreover, the man **Moses was exceedingly great in the land of Egypt, in the sight of Pharaoh's servants and of the people.***

2020 corresponding to the plague of darkness:

This mysterious event happened on May 21, 2020. The entire sky turned to pitch dark in the middle of the day within 10 mins of bright sunlight.

Daily star.co.uk 27 May 2020
Eerie moment Beijing sky turns pitch black in the middle of the day

The strange sight was recorded on the same day two annual conferences of the communist party started; leading some conspiracy theorists to bizarrely claim the footage was a sign from the heavens
BBC camera journalist Edward Lawrence says: "its 3.45 pm. Suddenly darkness has descended upon

Beijing.
"Literally 10 minutes ago it was pretty light and now it's this."Another wrote: "This is insane." While a third said: "That doesn't make any sense."

This is Beijing during the middle of the day on 21 May 2020: 3:45 pm.
The strange sight is believed to have been caused by a huge storm engulfing Beijing, with lightning seen moments before the video was taken.

 There is also another manifestation of this plague in 2020.

Exodus 10:23
The Egyptians could not see one another, nor did anyone rise from his place for three days; *but all the Israelites had natural light in their dwellings.*

This is exactly what the entire world went through during the lockdown and quarantine due to the Coronavirus. Millions of people were placed in quarantine where they couldn't see each other and their loved ones. People were trapped in their homes just like the Egyptians were trapped in their homes for 3 days. We didn't see our friends, relatives and co-workers during the time we were in quarantine. Billions of people are still in some form of lockdown where they are completely trapped inside their homes.

Before the final plague: The wealth transfer

Before the 10th and the final plague would be unleashed upon Egypt, there was one important thing yet to be done: the payment to the Israelites for the hard work and toil of 400 years was to be made.

Till now, the plagues had absolutely destroyed Egypt. The Egyptians had seen one after another, all of their gods being defeated and judged. They prayed to their gods, asked for help but none of the gods could deliver them from the plagues.

The Egyptians had lost fishes to the plague of Nile.

The Egyptians had lost livestock to the plague of pestilence.

The Egyptians had lost cattle to the plague of hailstones.

The Egyptians had lost barley and flax to the plague of hailstones.

The Egyptians had lost wheat and all the remaining crops to the plague of locust.

Their agriculture industry, fish industry and livestock industry were utterly destroyed. Their economy was destroyed. But still, the payment for the 400 years of hard work and toil was to be made for the judgement to be of any value to the Israelites. Without the payment for their works, it would have been pure revenge and not justice. Justice demands that the victim should be restored what he has lost and in this case, it was 400 years of hard work. The Israelites were slaves. Back then, slaves were not paid anything. They were just given enough food to survive. Servants are paid a wage, not slaves. In today's world, a lot of slaves are low waged employees because what they are paid is not enough to even survive. Many people have to take a second job and work 10-14 hours per day just to meet needs. How is it different from Egypt when the masters in Egypt provided enough food to only survive and today many employees only make enough money to barely survive? The only difference is that the masters in the past gave their slaves food and today the employers give only enough money to buy food. This is the modern day slavery. The time of justice has come.

Exodus 11:1-3
[1]THEN THE Lord said to Moses, Yet will I bring one plague more on Pharaoh and on Egypt; afterwards he will let you go. When he lets you go from here, he will thrust you out altogether.

[2]Speak now in the hearing of the people, and let every man solicit and ask of his neighbour, and every

*woman of her neighbour, **jewels of silver and jewels of gold.***

[3]And the Lord gave the people favour in the sight of the Egyptians. Moreover, the man Moses was exceedingly great in the land of Egypt, in the sight of Pharaoh's servants and of the people.

The wealth was transferred from the Egyptians to the Israelites. This was the payment for their centuries of hard work. Justice was made. The victims of slavery were restituted. The payment was made. Egypt: the richest nation of that time was not only destroyed but much of their gold and silver now belonged to the Israelites. The slaves had turned to millionaires. But justice was not complete yet. There was one sin committed by the Egyptians that was about to come back to haunt them. 80 years ago, they committed an abomination by killing thousands of innocent babies. It was time for justice.

Exodus 1:15-17, 22
[15]Then the king of Egypt said to the Hebrew midwives, of whom one was named Shiprah and the other Puah,
[16]When you act as midwives to the Hebrew women and see them on the birthstool, if it is a son, you shall kill him; but if it is a daughter, she shall live.
[17]But the midwives feared God and did not do as the king of Egypt commanded, but let the male babies live.
*[22]Then Pharaoh charged all his people, saying, **Every son born [to the Hebrews] you shall cast***

into the river [Nile], *but every daughter you shall allow to live.*

Even Moses was almost killed due to this verdict of the old king of Egypt. We do not know for how long was this law executed in Egypt but we do know that by the time Moses was born this rule was a norm and now at the time of the plagues, Moses was 80 years old. Due to continued demand for labour, this law might have been discontinued later but there is a great possibility that for decades innocent male sons of the Israelites were thrown into the river and killed. If we consider the population of Israelites at that time which is supposed to be three million, hundreds of thousands of innocent children were murdered by the Egyptians.

Justice had to be served. The blood of thousands of babies was on the hands of the Egyptians. Their blood cried out to God. God had to do justice.

Genesis 4:10
Berean Study Bible
"What have you done?" replied the LORD. "The voice of your brother's blood cries out to Me from the ground.

This is the reason for the dreaded final plague in which it is said that there was not a house in Egypt that was not mourning.

Exodus 12:30
English Standard Version

And Pharaoh rose up in the night, he and all his servants and all the Egyptians. And there was a great cry in Egypt, for **there was not a house where someone was not dead.**

But the final plague was still to be unleashed. Pharaoh had not yet permitted Israel to leave Egypt with all their belongings. This is the reason why God hardened the heart of Pharaoh that he didn't allow Israel to leave for if he allowed Israel to leave after the first plague, there would be no justice for the blood of thousands of innocent babies.

Now let's come to 2020

Here we are in the 21st century and looks likes the world has not changed a bit. We are guilty of the same crimes that the Egyptians committed. The Egyptians were judged for two crimes that they committed: the killing of innocent newly born babies and oppressive slavery. Today in 2020, we are guilty of both.

The world is guilty of something same today that the Egyptians were guilty of and that is probably the reason why all of this has come upon the entire world. 3500 years ago, only Egypt was guilty but today all of us are. We never learn from history. If they couldn't run away from the judgements of their sins, why do we think that we can?

Abortion:

Here is a small display of our society:

According to WHO, every year in the world there are an estimated 40-50 million abortions. This corresponds to approximately 125,000 abortions per day.

In the USA, where nearly half of pregnancies are unintended and four in 10 of these are terminated by abortion, there are over 3,000 abortions per day. Twenty-two percent of all pregnancies in the USA (excluding miscarriages) end in abortion.

How are we guiltless? Are we not guilty? If killing babies just born is a crime then killing an innocent soul inside the womb is a crime too. If the Egyptians couldn't escape the punishment for killing hundreds of thousands of innocent babies, will we escape the punishment for killing millions of innocent babies?

Is God judging the world? Not yet. But probably, the sins of the past might return in the future to haunt the ones who committed them.

The black slavery

Genesis 15:13
New International Version
Then the LORD said to him, "Know for certain that for **four hundred years** *your descendants will be*

*strangers in a country not their own and that they will be **enslaved and mistreated there.***

Is it a coincidence that 2019-2020 was chosen for the plagues? Why not any other year? Is it a random occurrence that out of any year that could have been chosen for "black lives matter" protest, 2020 was chosen? Crimes against the blacks have been committed for centuries and this is definitely not the first time that a black man has been murdered by the Police. But the protest took place in 2020, 400 years after the first black slave arrival in the US.

In 1619, the first black slaves entered America. After four hundred years they are still enslaved and mistreated. The only difference is that in the past they were direct slaves and today they are economic slaves. In the past, these slaves were given food to be alive and today they are given enough money to buy food themselves. That's the only difference. They are one of the lowest wage earners in society. The income inequality between white and black is unfathomable.

In 2019, 400 years of black slavery is completed. The time for restoration has come. For 400 years, Israelites were slaved and for the last 400 years, the blacks have been enslaved economically. It's time for their deliverance. It's time to set them free. That's why we are seeing "black lives matter" protest in 2020. It's not just a coincidence. Blacks are murdered every year all around the US but why has this case of George Floyd turned to a global phenomenon in 2020? Nothing happens without a reason. Everything happens with a purpose. There is a reason why black lives matter protest is happening even in the middle of the Coronavirus pandemic. This was destined to happen. It's time that the black Americans are set free.

Plague 10: The final plague: the death of the firstborn

Exodus 12:21-23, 28-33
[21]Then Moses called for all the elders of Israel, and said to them, Go forth, select and take a lamb according to your families and kill the Passover [lamb].
[22]And you shall take a bunch of hyssop, dip it in the blood in the basin, and touch the lintel above the door and the two side posts with the blood; and none of you shall go out of his house until morning.
[23]For the Lord will pass through to slay the Egyptians; and when He sees the blood upon the lintel and the two side posts, the Lord will pass over the door and will not allow the destroyer to come into your houses to slay you.
[28]The Israelites went and, as the Lord had commanded Moses and Aaron, so they did.
[29]At midnight the Lord slew every firstborn in the land of Egypt, from the firstborn of Pharaoh who sat on his throne to the firstborn of the prisoner in the dungeon, and all the firstborn of the livestock.
[30]Pharaoh rose up in the night, he, all his servants, and all the Egyptians; and there was a great cry in Egypt, for there was not a house where there was not one dead.

*[31]He called for Moses and Aaron by night, and said, Rise up, get out from among my people, both you and the Israelites; and go, serve the Lord, as you said.
[32]Also take your flocks and your herds, as you have said, and be gone! And [ask your God to] bless me also.
[33]The Egyptians were urgent with the people to depart, that they might send them out of the land in haste; for they said, We are all dead men.*

This was the final plague. After this plague, Pharaoh not only allowed the Israelites to go, he thrust them away. He had enough of all the plagues and he finally let the Israelites go. This plague was a direct attack on Pharaoh. In ancient Egypt, Pharaoh was considered a god himself and there were other dummy gods who were protectors of Pharaoh. But none of them including Pharaoh could save his son who was going to be the next Pharaoh from death. This was the final punishment on Egyptians for killing innocent Hebrew babies. The old King of Egypt had killed Jewish babies and God killed the firstborn male child of both Egyptian men and of their remaining livestock.

The final plague occurred on the night of the first Passover. The Israelites were going to be delivered the next day. They still celebrate the day of their freedom and deliverance as Passover. On Passover after 1500 years, Jesus was crucified as the sacrifice for our sins. Just like in the night of Passover, the blood of the lamb protected everyone who entered the doors painted with blood; the blood of Jesus protects anyone who comes under the protection of his blood. That's why Jesus died on the Passover. It is said that many Egyptians who feared the Lord took their children to the houses of Israelites. Everyone who took refuge in the houses covered by blood was spared from the coming destruction. It's the same today that anyone who is covered by the blood of Jesus is spared from destruction today.

2020 corresponding to the final plague

On the night of the first Passover, every Israelite was inside their house. 3500 years later, in 2020 every Jewish all over the world are under lockdown and quarantine. They are locked inside their houses just like they were 3500 years ago. It looks like history is repeating itself. A plague was seeking whom to devour then and a plague is seeking whom to devour today.

But this is not the only resemblance. The plague killed only the firstborn which is similar to what is happening today. The Coronavirus is disproportionately killing the firstborn among us that is the elderly. While the elderly are at the biggest risk with a majority of diseases, it's not always the case. In 1920 Spanish flu, the young and healthy were disproportionately harmed due to a strong immune response that attacked their own bodies. The Spanish flu pandemic mostly killed young adults. In 1918–1919, 99% of pandemic influenza deaths in the U.S. occurred in people under 65, and nearly half of deaths were in young adults: 20 to 40 years old. But this time, during the Coronavirus the elderly are the most harmed by the virus although both the pandemics are compared to be similar. Why didn't this virus affect the young people more like the Spanish flu? The elderly who are the firstborn among us are disproportionately affected by the Coronavirus.

God of Israel VS the gods of Egypt

The Egyptians were very religious people. They had gods for everything. They had 39 main gods; many of them depicted in Egyptian art with animal bodies or heads and approx 2000 deities in total. Many animals were considered sacred in ancient Egypt.

Israel had lived in Egypt for 400 years and had been infiltrated with Egyptian culture. Taking Egypt out of the hearts and minds of the Israelites was equally important as taking the Israelites out of Egypt. The plagues were an attack on the gods and goddess of Egypt which would remove any doubt in the minds of the Israelites as to who was the true God. God had in mind not only to take His people out of Egypt but to discourage worship of the idols.

The 10 plagues were not judgement only to the Egyptians; it was an attack on Egyptian dummy gods. So it is important to see the plagues with this perspective too. There were around 2000 deities worshipped in ancient Egypt but the judgement was on all the main gods that were worshipped.

Exodus 12:12
New Living Translation
On that night I will pass through the land of Egypt and strike down every firstborn son and firstborn male animal in the land of Egypt. ***I will execute judgment against all the gods of Egypt, for I am the LORD!***

Numbers 33:3-4
On the fifteenth day of the first month, on the day after the Passover, the Israelites set out from Rameses. They marched out triumphantly in full view of all the Egyptians, 4who were burying all their firstborn, whom the LORD had struck down among them; for ***the LORD had executed judgment against their gods***

The battle was not just between God and the Egyptians; it was between the gods of Egypt and the LORD. It was the judgement on their gods. It was as if the Lord was challenging the people of Egypt saying. "Let your god save you if they can".

Egyptians were polytheist in their religious cultures. They worshipped everything from the sun to rivers to

Pharaoh. This was unacceptable to the creator GOD that these Egyptians were worshipping the creation rather than the creator.

The plagues were a sign that the LORD, God of Israel was far greater than all of the multiple Gods of the Egyptians. Every Egyptian plague was unleashed corresponding to the ancient gods and goddesses that were prevalent during that time. Polytheism was very common during that time. A lot of tribes in the nearby land of Cannan or ancient Mesopotamia used to worship multiple gods and goddesses. Egypt was the superpower and the most developed and powerful nation at that time: Similar to the USA today or British Empire 200 years ago. The plagues were a display of power not only to Egypt but the entire known world and nearby kingdoms who worshipped multiple gods and goddesses. The judgement was unleashed upon a king: Pharaoh who considered himself as God.

Exodus 7:3

*I multiply my signs and wonders in Egypt, 4 he will not listen to you. Then I will lay my hand on Egypt and with mighty acts of judgment I will bring out my divisions, my people the Israelites. 5 **And the Egyptians will know that I am the Lord** when I stretch out my hand against Egypt and bring the Israelites out of it."*

A few years later, this was said by a resident of a nearby tribe in the land of Canaan who heard about the display of Lord's power on Egypt:

Joshua 2:10-11
For we have heard how the LORD made a dry path for you through the Red Sea when you left Egypt. And we know what you did to Sihon and Og, the two Amorite kings east of the Jordan River, whose people you completely destroyed.
When we heard this, our hearts melted and everyone's courage failed because of you, for the LORD your God is God in the heavens above and on the earth below

When Moses went to Pharaoh and demanded that he let go of the people of Israel so that they may serve the Lord. This is what Pharaoh replied:

Exodus 5:1-2

*After that, Moses and Aaron went to Pharaoh and said, "This is what the LORD, the God of Israel, says: 'Let My people go, so that they may hold a feast to Me in the wilderness.' "But Pharaoh replied, "**Who is the LORD that I should obey His voice and let Israel go? I do not know the LORD, and I will not let Israel go.**"*

This bluntness was the beginning of the plagues.

Plagues of Egypt corresponding to the gods of Egypt:

There were 10 plagues unleashed upon Egypt. Each plague was aimed on the gods of Egypt. It was a challenge to each of the corresponding gods. Number 10 in the Bible denotes perfection and 10 plagues denote the completion of his judgement on Egypt. When the Lord turned the Nile to blood, it was a challenge on the Egyptian god of Nile and Egyptian god of fishes. Similarly, all the 10 plagues were direct attacks on almost all of the major Egyptian gods.

The First Plague: the Nile turns to Blood

Egyptian god Khnum: giver and guardian of the Nile River.

Egyptian god Hatmehit: guardian goddess of fish and fishermen.

Egyptian god Osiris: god of the underworld.

Egyptian god Sodpet and Satet

Egyptian god Hapi: Egyptian god of the Nile

The first plague was turning the water into blood. This plague was the direct attack on Hapi: the Egyptian god of Nile. Hapi was greatly celebrated among the Egyptians. Some of the titles of Hapi were "Lord of the Fish" and "Lord of the River Bringing Vegetation". Due to his fertile nature, he was sometimes considered the "father of the gods" This legend that is still widely believed by Egyptians, says that during Pharaonic times an important festival was celebrated in Egypt, where a young virgin was chosen from among the most beautiful women in the land and was thrown into the Nile as a sacrifice to the river god Hapi. Sacrificing a young girl as human sacrifice is an abomination to the Lord. This makes the judgement on Hapi god of Egypt rightful and justified.

Human sacrifice is a huge abomination to the LORD.

Egypt was a desert country, and its economy and livelihood depended on the Nile. Its crops were irrigated by the Nile, and its fields depended on fertile soil washed in by the river. The Nile was also the primary "highway" for the country: much of its trade and commerce depended on it.

When the river turned to blood, Hapi who was also called the lord of fishes could not save the fishes of Nile. The same bloody water through canals reached the vegetation and crops and affected them but Hapi couldn't save the vegetation either.

The Egyptians' supply of water for drinking, bathing and washing was now a toxic mess. The fishes, one of their major food sources, were wiped out. This was utterly devastating to the country.

The Nile was so important to the Egyptians; they worshipped several gods who were responsible for watching over it. The great god Khnum, usually represented as a human male with a ram's head, was viewed as the giver and guardian of the Nile River.

Egyptian god Hapi was credited with the annual Nile flood that brought in thousands of tons of fresh topsoil to re fertilize the land every year. Also linked to the Nile floodwaters were the gods Sodpet and Satet.

One of Egypt's trinity of greatest gods was Osiris, the god of the underworld. The Egyptians viewed the Nile River as his bloodstream: and now it was literally like blood. You can imagine the horror in the hearts of the Egyptians as they looked on the formerly beautiful and life-sustaining river that was now a giant stinking pool with tons of dead and rotting fish lining the shores. This struck also at Hatmehit, guardian goddess of fish and fishermen.

For 7 days, the Nile remained bloody: short enough that entire Egypt was not wiped out but long enough to send entire Egypt into a panic. The first plague was a clear message to all the Egypt that the war was on. Because all the waters in the containers were also turned to blood, this plague caused serious drinking water issues in Egypt. All the surface water was turned to blood probably affecting even the Israelites so God gave a chance of survival in the form of underground water.

Exodus 7:24
And all the Egyptians dug along the Nile to get drinking water, because they could not drink the water of the river.

The servants of Pharaoh through their secret magic could also turn water to blood but couldn't change the blood water back to normal water.

The Second Plague: Frogs coming from the Nile River

Egyptian goddess Heket: goddess of Fertility, Water and Renewal

Heqet (Heqat, Heket) was the goddess of childbirth and fertility in Ancient Egypt. She was depicted as a frog or a woman with the head of a frog. In Egypt, Frogs symbolized fruitfulness and new life. Frogs were viewed as sacred in Egypt because they lived in two worlds: in water and on land. They were considered so sacred that killing them was punishable by death.

In this plague literally millions and millions of frogs were overflowing the land and killing one by stepping on it was punishable by death, yet how could that be avoided? There were frogs on the ground, frogs in the houses, frogs on their beds, frogs in their cooking ovens and frogs in their bowls.

The Egyptians literally could not walk without stepping on frogs and squashing them that they believed to be sacred. But in so doing they were violating their own laws and sentencing themselves to death for offending the goddess Heqet and these other frog deities. Pharaoh called Moses and asked him to pray to the Lord to remove the frogs. God answered their prayers and all the frogs died. The people who worshipped these frogs had to now deal with millions of dead frogs all around them. Finally, the people had to go out to gather them into great mounds of decaying, stinking frogs: so much for their sacred animal.

The Third Plague: Gnats (lice or mosquitoes)

Egyptian god Geb: the god of the earth.

This object of this plague is still debated. Some say its lice and others say its mosquitoes. In any of the cases, this plague was directed at Geb, the god of the earth. Egyptians gave offerings to Geb for the bounty of the land—but in this case, rather than the land bringing forth crops and fruit and vegetables, it brought forth itching, biting gnats. And their god Geb was shown to be powerless to prevent it. Egyptians invoked Har-pa-khered (Horus in child form) to ward off dangerous creatures and Imhotep as the god of medicinal healing as well as other healing gods, but there was no relief. Pharaoh too was considered a god yet he was personally afflicted with the gnats.

The Fourth Plague: Swarms of flies

Egyptian god Kheper
Egyptian god Amun: god of the wind

The "swarms" in this passage is also debated. Some say its wild animals, others say it is gadflies. Most scholars agree that these were swarms of some flying and crawling insect. The Egyptian god Kheper was depicted as a man with a dung beetle in place of his head. Kheper was viewed as the god who pushed the sun across the sky. He was associated with the dung beetle because dung beetles would roll manure into spherical balls and push these around on the ground, similar to how the Egyptians thought Kheper pushed the sun across the sky. Kheper was shown to be incapable of controlling the highly destructive insects that were destroying Egypt. We might also note the supreme god Amun, the god of the wind, who should have been able to blow the swarms away was helpless.

This is the first plague in which God made a distinction between His people and the Egyptians.

The Fifth Plague: Pestilence

Creation god Ptah
Creator sun gods Atum and Re
Creation goddesses Nut and Neith goddesses Hathor

This plague created an enormous economic disaster for the Egyptians. It affected their food, transportation, military capability, farming capacity and economic goods that were produced by these cattle. Cattle in Egypt were not just highly valued, they were also considered sacred. The Egyptians worshipped many animals, and among them were bulls and heifers. The creation god Ptah was represented by a living bull known as the Apis bull. The creator sun god Atum and Re, blended as the same deity, was represented by the black bull. Sky and creation goddesses Nut and Neith were depicted as a celestial cow. One of Egypt's greatest mother goddesses was Hathor, depicted as a cow-headed goddess or a female with cow-like features. In this plague, these various gods of Egypt were powerless to protect the cattle and livestock of the Egyptians. Keep in mind that as each plague was sent, the Egyptians probably desperately prayed to their gods to stop the plagues. But in every case, their gods were powerless and silent.

The Sixth Plague: Boils

Egyptian god Imhotep: god of medicine
Egyptian god Thoth: god of intelligence and medical learning.
Egyptian god Nefertem: god of healing.

The Egyptians worshipped several healing deities, on occasion even sacrificing human beings to them. The victims were burned on an altar, and their ashes were cast into the air, where the wind would blow the ashes over the people. This was viewed as a blessing for them. Moses took ashes from the furnace and threw them into the air. This furnace represents the hard toil and slavery of the Israelites. The ashes were scattered by the wind and fell on all the priests, people and the animals that were left. But rather than a blessing, this turned into painful boils—large sores on the people.

Priests with their magical powers, especially those in the cult of Sekhmet, yet another goddess of healing besides her major role as a war goddess, were the doctors of ancient Egypt. However, the magicians suffered so horribly from the boils that they could barely stand, let alone use the power of their apparently powerless gods to heal others: They couldn't even heal themselves

The Seventh Plague: Hailstones and lightning

Egyptian god Nut, the sky goddess
Egyptian god Shu, the god of air and bearer of heaven
Egyptian god Seth, the god of storms and protector of crops
Egyptian god Neper, the god of grain crops
Egyptian god Osiris, the ruler of life and vegetation

Next came the plague of hail. This would have been very unusual, as the region where this took place receives only about two inches of rain per year.

This plague was another devastating attack on the country. The Egyptians had already lost fish from their diet when the Nile turned to blood. The plague on the livestock killed off much of it, and animals still in the field at the time of this hailstorm were killed by the hail, so the Egyptians have now lost much of their sources of meat and milk. And still, the various cow deities mentioned earlier could do nothing. Not only that, Nepher: god of crops couldn't save crops, Seth: god of storms couldn't stop storms and Osiris: ruler of life and vegetation couldn't save cattle and crops.

The Eighth Plague: Locusts

Egyptian god Anubis: guardian of the fields

Egyptian god Osiris: chief agricultural god
Egyptian god Amun: god of the wind
Egyptian god Shu: god of the air

The plague of hail had wiped out the crops and most plants, but the little that had survived would now be devoured by locusts.

Locusts can fly up to 150 km daily and a one square km swarm can eat as much food as 35,000 people in terms of weight in a single day. This was not a normal swarm of Locusts, this was a plague. It was sent so that no green thing would be left in Egypt. A great west wind blew locust into Egypt and a great West wind took away locust from Egypt when Moses prayed to God to deliver from locust.

Amin: god of wind couldn't stop the Lord from blowing strong West wind that brought Locusts to Egypt and Osiris: the god of vegetation couldn't save crops.

The Ninth Plague: Darkness

The Egyptian sun god Ra

Imagine, what would happen if the sun doesn't rise up tomorrow? We can't even imagine the panic that was upon the people of Egypt. Imagine how they would have felt in complete darkness for 3 days. Today we have so many inventions like bulbs and LEDs, so we might not understand what they went through. But imagine how they would have felt because those were the times before the light bulb was invented. They didn't know that darkness would be over by 3 days. Imagine, the Egyptians thought that darkness would be over by tomorrow morning but it doesn't. This goes on for a day and a night. Then it continues for another day and night. Then a third day and night. For people used to bright sunshine 365 days a year, this had to be terrifying. By the end of 3 days, they would have lost all hopes of seeing life again. And this darkness was palpable—you can somehow feel it pressing in on you from all around.

Of all the gods of Egypt, none were worshipped as much as the sun. The sun god variously known as Re, Ra, Atum or Aten (and sometimes Horus) had become identified with the supreme god Amun, Amon or Amen. Amon-Ra was thus considered the greatest of the gods of Egypt. He was viewed as the creator, the giver of life, who flooded the land with his energizing rays.

But in this darkness Amon-Ra was silent. He was nowhere to be seen, literally. Nothing was visible in the smothering darkness that covered the land. Not only were all of Egypt's other gods and goddesses powerless but their greatest and most important god, Amon-Ra, was just as powerless and useless to help them. Again the Egyptians' gods had failed them.

By this time, the people of Egypt had enough of the plagues.

Exodus 10:7

And Pharaoh's servants said unto him, How long shall this man be a snare unto us? let the men go, that they may serve the LORD their God: know you not yet that Egypt is destroyed?

The Tenth Plague: the death of the firstborn

Pharaoh: son of Ra
Egyptian god Serket: the goddess of protection
Egyptian god Sobek: the god of protection and fertility

With this plague, the Egyptian pharaoh finally relented and let the Israelites go. This forcing of Pharaoh to act against his will would demonstrate God's overthrow of his sovereignty and of the gods who represented it: Hu: the god personifying royal authority; Wadjet: the goddess of royal authority; Maat: goddess of cosmic order under whose aegis the rulers of Egypt governed; and the war goddess Sekhmet: who would supposedly breathe fire against the enemies of the pharaoh.

The Egyptian god Meshkenet, the goddess who presided at the birth of children, failed to save the firstborn. Renenutet, the special protector god of the pharaoh, could not protect the pharaoh's son who would be the next pharaoh. Osiris, the giver and ruler of life couldn't save death from covering Egypt. There was death in every house in Egypt. Yet none of these dummy god's could save them. Where was the war goddess Sekhmet, when the Lord declared war on Egyptian gods and defeated them? Why was she so helpless before the Lord?

Pharaoh was defeated along with all his dummy gods and goddesses. Pharaoh who considered himself god couldn't save his child from death. The Lord made an open mockery and a public spectacle of the Egyptian gods and goddesses. By now, the Egyptians and the Israelites both knew who the Lord was.

The plagues began after Pharaoh bluntly declared, "Who is this Lord that I should obey him. I do not know the Lord and I will not let Israel go ". The plagues ended when Pharaoh accepted his defeat and allowed Israel to go. By now not only Pharaoh but all of Egypt and Israel knew who the Lord was and why should they obey him.

With this I would like to end this book. Thank you so much for reading. Your feedbacks means a lot to us, so if you found this book helpful, please let us know your thoughts. Feel free to mail us at: **thetenplagues2020@gmail.com**

Thank you for reading this book

Disclaimer

No advice

You are responsible for your own actions and behavior, and none of this book is to be considered legal, personal or medical advice.

You accept full responsibility and liability for actions and results from using any products, services or suggestions made inside this book and its supplemental resources.

The information in this book is not advice and should not be treated as advice.

You must not rely on the information in the book as an alternative to [legal] OR [medical] OR [financial] OR [*spiritual*] advice from an appropriately qualified professional. If you have any specific questions about any such matter you should consult an appropriately qualified professional.

If you think you may be suffering from any medical condition you should seek immediate medical attention. You should never delay seeking medical advice, disregard medical advice, or discontinue medical treatment because of information in the book.

You should never delay seeking legal advice, disregard legal advice, or commence or discontinue any legal action because of information in the book.

Limited warranties

Whilst we endeavor to ensure that the information in the book is correct, we do not warrant or represent its completeness or accuracy.

We do not warrant or represent that the use of the book will lead to any particular outcome or result.[In particular, we do not warrant or represent that by using the book you will *[not get infected with the Coronavirus or be successful in your business].*] Our intention is to share with you principles important for godly living. Please consult an actual professional for advice.

To the maximum extent permitted by applicable law, we exclude all representations, warranties and conditions relating to this book and the use of this book.

Limitations and exclusions of liability

Nothing in this disclaimer will:

> (a) Limit or exclude any liability for death or personal injury resulting from negligence;
>
> (b) Limit or exclude any liability for fraud or fraudulent misrepresentation;
>
> (c) Limit any liabilities in any way that is not permitted under applicable law;

(d)   Exclude any liabilities that may not be excluded under applicable law; or

(e)   Limit or exclude any mandatory rights that you have as a consumer under applicable law.

The limitations and exclusions of liability set out in this disclaimer:

(a)   Are subject to the preceding provision; and

(b)   Govern all liabilities arising under this disclaimer or relating to the subject matter of this disclaimer, including liabilities arising in contract, in tort (including negligence) and for breach of statutory duty, except to the extent expressly provided otherwise in this disclaimer.

We will not be liable to you in respect of any losses arising out of any event or events beyond our reasonable control.

We will not be liable to you in respect of any business losses, including (without limitation) loss of or damage to profits, income, revenue, use, production, anticipated savings, business, contracts, commercial opportunities or goodwill.

We will not be liable to you in respect of any loss or corruption of any data, database or software.

We will not be liable to you in respect of any special, indirect or consequential loss or damage.

Thank you for reading this book.

If you found this book helpful, please let us know your thoughts. Feel free to mail us at: **thetenplagues2020@gmail.com**